# If Wishes Were Horses

## A KONA STORY

By Sibley Miller

Illustrated by Tara Larsen Chang and Jo Gershman

Feiwel and Friends

For Paul and Mira—Sibley Miller

For Zoe, who remains my favorite "fairy walk" companion
—Tara Larsen Chang

For Kandis and Sherry of Roze-El Stables,
for opening my door to the world of horses
—Jo Gershman

## A FEIWEL AND FRIENDS BOOK
An Imprint of Macmillan

WIND DANCERS: IF WISHES WERE HORSES. Copyright © 2008 by Reeves International, Inc. All rights reserved. BREYER, WIND DANCERS, and BREYER logos are trademarks and/or registered trademarks of Reeves International, Inc. Printed in China. For information, address Feiwel and Friends, 175 Fifth Avenue, New York, N.Y. 10010.

Library of Congress Cataloging-in-Publication Data

Miller, Sibley.
If wishes were horses : a Kona story / by Sibley Miller.
p. cm. — (Wind Dancers ; bk. #1)
Summary: Four tiny, flying horses suddenly come into being, blown out of a dandelion by a lonely girl, and set out to discover who they are and what they are supposed to do with their magical powers.
ISBN-13: 978-0-312-38280-3 / ISBN-10: 0-312-38280-4
[1. Magic—Fiction. 2. Horses—Fiction. 3. Loneliness—Fiction.] I. Title.
PZ7.M63373If 2008   [E]—dc22   2008012784

DESIGNED BY BARBARA GRZESLO
Feiwel and Friends logo designed by Filomena Tuosto

First Edition: November 2008

1  3  5  7  9  10  8  6  4  2

www.feiwelandfriends.com

# CONTENTS

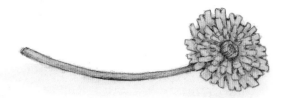

## A Doozy of a Dandelion

The pretty meadow behind Leanna's yellow farmhouse and big red barn had wildflowers, trees, animals, and insects. Yet, Leanna didn't feel happy in her new home.

"All I've got are a bunch of birds and bees, dragonflies and dandelions," Leanna said to herself. "No friends yet."

Just then, one of the meadow's many dandelions brushed against her leg. Leanna looked down at it in surprise. This dandelion was a doozy! It was very tall and its bloom was as big as a hen's egg.

With some effort, Leanna broke its stem. Then—because what else do you do with a dandelion?—she took a breath, and blew.

The dandelion unleashed a storm of seeds. But some of them—four, to be exact—didn't look like dandelion seeds at all.

They looked, amazingly, like . . . horses!

Like very tiny horses. Very tiny *flying* horses! Horses with sparkling wings.

Leanna gasped and began running after the little, fluttering creatures.

One of the horses was tawny pink with coral and turquoise wings. Another had a lovely sea-green mane and tail. A third looked like sunlight, all gold and orange. And the last had a violet-black coat, with pretty white socks on her front legs.

As the horses flew upward, they looked like they were dancing on the wind.

"Oh!" Leanna cried. "You're so pretty!"

But the horses didn't seem to hear her. Instead, they flew on, whinnying happily.

Then, suddenly—like soap bubbles that had popped—they disappeared.

"Where'd they go?" Leanna whispered to herself, squinting up at the sky.

*Maybe I just dreamed them up,* she thought, biting her lip.

But then Leanna looked at the dandelion stem, still clutched in her fist.

"I *know* they were real," she said aloud.

She peered into the sky one last time, wondering why the horses had disappeared. She wondered, too, if she would ever see them again.

## CHAPTER 1
# Dancing on the Wind

The first thing the tiny winged horse heard was a *whooshing* of wind in her ears.

The first thing she felt was a breeze ruffling her long purple mane.

The first thing she smelled? The grass and sun-kissed flowers.

But the best part of the filly's very first moments were the things she saw. Because what she saw were colors. *Her* colors.

The violet-black and white of her front legs, pumping through the air.

The shimmery purple of her wings. The

bright tiny flowers that danced around her.

The little horse tossed her head and whinnied in excitement. But when the whinny came out, it was a word—"Kona!"

"Kona?" the little filly heard someone ask. "What's a Kona?"

The voice came from behind her. With a flicker of her wings, the horse turned in the air. And that's when she saw the most wonderful thing of all—one, no two, no *three* other tiny flying horses just like herself!

Each had colorful wings and long, shiny manes and tails, just like she did.

But they were different, too. One of the two fillies was silvery blue, with sea-green wings. The other one was the prettiest sunset pink, with a necklace of glimmering jewels.

The last of the winged horses, surprisingly, was a colt! He was long legged and fiery gold. Everywhere he flew, a halo of colorful

little butterflies bobbled around him.

"Well?" the colt demanded. "Like I asked before—what's a Kona?"

The violet-black horse cocked her head to think. Finally, she announced, "I think a Kona is . . . me! Kona must be my name!"

"Really?" asked the silver-blue filly. "How do you know?"

"I . . . I just *do*!" Kona said with a smile.

"Then can you tell me *my* name?" the pretty pink horse asked. "I don't know it."

"I bet you *do* know your name," Kona assured her. "You just don't *know* that you know it!"

"Huh?" said the silver-blue filly. "So does that mean *I* know my name, too?"

"Just close your eyes," Kona told her new friends. She didn't know if this was going to work. But since she'd been the first one to figure out *her* name, she pressed on.

"Now, feel the wind breezing through your mane," Kona ordered.

"Hee!" The pink horse giggled. "That tickles!"

"Now, smell the sun on the grass," Kona went on.

The golden horse's nostrils flared as he inhaled deeply. In fact, he breathed in so much air, he sucked in a gnat! He coughed, and finally sneezed the gnat out.

Kona tried not to laugh as she gave the other horses her next instruction: "Now, say the first word that comes to you."

The sleek silver-blue horse's eyes popped
open. "Sumatra!" she
cried out joyously.
"Sumatra! That's
my name! I just
*know* it!"

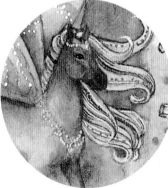

"That's an elegant
name!" said the pink
horse. "Want to know mine?"

"Of course," Sumatra said.

"It's Brisa," the coral-
pink filly answered, as
she ducked her head
shyly. "I think it's a
very pretty name,
don't you?"

"I've got mine!"
the golden horse
interrupted. "Apple Pie!"

"Apple Pie?" Sumatra said. "I think that's a dessert, not a horse's name."

"What can I tell you?" the colt said. "It's what popped into my head. I must be hungry!"

"Maybe," Kona suggested gently, "you should try again."

"Okay," the golden horse agreed. He squeezed his eyes shut and concentrated.

Finally, he let out an explosive breath and, with it, a word: "Sirocco!"

He opened his eyes.

"That's it! That's it! Sirocco!" he brayed triumphantly. He looked down at the meadow and waved his hoof. "Hello, down there? My name's Sirocco!"

"Who are you talking to?" Kona asked.

The three fillies glanced downward. They saw a young girl standing alone, looking puzzled. She was holding a dandelion stem and peering up into the sky. She looked nice, but sad.

Kona used her own hoof to wave to the girl. As she did, she noticed that the halo of flowers dancing around her waved as well!

But the girl didn't seem to notice, because she called out, "Come back!"

"No problem!" Sirocco replied. Batting his wings extra hard, he darted downward until he fluttered a few feet above the girl's head.

But the girl still didn't react.

"You guys," Kona said breathlessly. "This is really strange. That girl? I don't think she can see us! And I don't know why!"

## CHAPTER 2
# A *Big* Surprise

"What do you mean she can't see us?"
Sumatra gazed at the girl in the dandelion
meadow. "We're *right here*!"

"Weird!" Sirocco said with a nicker.

"Maybe," Kona added thoughtfully,
"*weird* isn't the word for it."

"But it *is* weird," Brisa insisted. "How can
that girl ignore us when we're so pretty?"

To emphasize her point, Brisa spun in the
air. The jewels on her halo shone like a
necklace, and her blond mane
shimmered.

Kona swallowed a laugh and said, "I don't think she *means* to ignore us. But something's making us invisible to her."

"Invisible!" Sirocco said. His eyes went wide. "Does that mean we're ghosts?"

"No," Kona said excitedly. "More like something . . . enchanted. You know, like fairies."

"Oh, please," Sumatra snorted. "What's so enchanted about flying horses?"

"Okay," Kona challenged her. She pointed at a woodpecker flying nearby. "Check out that bird. Do you notice anything about him?"

"He flies," Sumatra noted, "just like us."

"But do you see what's *different* from us?" Kona asked.

Sumatra shrugged.

"There are no butterflies or flowers dancing around

 him," Kona said, answering her own question and motioning at the halos that surrounded Sirocco and herself. "No ribbons or jewels either," she added, pointing at Sumatra's and Brisa's halos.

Sumatra gasped. For the first time, she noticed that a ring of fluttering ribbons was floating around her, following her every move. Brisa, too, saw that she was surrounded by a halo of jewels.

"You're right!" Brisa squealed.

"So," Sumatra asked, "do you think it's these halos that are making us invisible?"

"I do," Kona said. As she nodded, she spotted a horse paddock on the far edge of the dandelion meadow.

"Look!" Kona said to her pals. "There are more of us over there!"

"Do you think the little girl can see *them*?" Sumatra wondered.

"Let's go over and ask 'em," Sirocco said.

The four tiny horses took off. But as they approached the paddock, Kona frowned. Something about these horses wasn't right. To start with—they had no wings!

What's more, the horses were *enormous*.

"What kind of strange horses are they?" Sumatra asked her friends.

She asked the question so loudly that one of the wingless horses—a pretty chestnut mare munching on hay—pricked up her ears and snorted.

"I should ask *you* pip-squeaks the same thing," she said. "I've heard of miniature horses, but this is ridiculous!"

"Hey!" Sirocco said. "Who are you calling ridiculous?"

Before the mare could answer, a gelding galloped over.

"Those are the weirdest-looking flies I've ever seen!" he whinnied to the mare. "Want me to get 'em with my tail?"

He raised his giant, brushy black tail.

*"Eeek!"* Brisa neighed. She flew to Kona and hid behind her. "He's going to swat us!"

At the sound of Brisa's frightened whinny, the gelding cocked his head.

"Hey, those little buzzy things are *horses*," he said to the mare.

Kona cringed. These huge horses didn't seem to like them very much. But Kona needed answers. So, she politely pressed on.

"Sorry to bother you," she said, "but are *you* invisible to girls like we are?"

"Are you kidding?" The gelding laughed. "Not only can girls see us, they *love* us. They feed us and brush our coats and ride us. Too bad you're too puny—not to mention invisible—for all that!"

Now, a spotted gray filly trotted over.

"So *what* if they are puny," she said to the gelding. "*I* think they're neat. I wouldn't mind being invisible myself every now and then."

Then she turned to Kona and her friends.

"You guys aren't like any horses *I've* ever

seen," she said admiringly. "You *fly*."

"Well, sure!" Sirocco said. "How else are we supposed to get around?"

"Young fellow," the mare said haughtily, "horses walk. Or canter, trot, or gallop. We even jump. But horses do *not* fly."

"Then what does that make us?" Sumatra demanded.

"I'm sure I don't know," the mare said. "And I don't care to help a huffy one like you figure it out, either!"

Turning around abruptly, the mare, and

then the gelding, strutted back to the other side of the paddock.

But the young gray filly stayed put. She gazed up at Kona and her friends.

"I think I know what you are," she whispered. "I think you're . . . *enchanted*."

"Wow!" said Brisa, exchanging delighted grins with her friends. "Kona was right!"

"No wonder the little girl can't see us," Sirocco yelled joyously. "We're no ordinary horses. We're *magic*!"

CHAPTER 3
# Magic in the Air

"I can't believe we're magic!" Sumatra shouted.

"We're totally unique!" Brisa cried. She spun around in the air.

"I'm king of the world!" Sirocco crowed, doing a backflip.

"Well, let's not get carried away," Kona said.

Sirocco stopped, mid-flip.

"Are you telling me that you're not *excited* about being magic?" he demanded of Kona.

"Of *course* I'm excited!" Kona said. "But I'm also curious. I mean, what do *magic* horses do? Why are we here? What's our purpose?"

"I have a question of my own," Sirocco said. "What would be more fun? Talking about what we do, or going off and doing it?"

Flitting her wings, Brisa rose high above the others and gazed down at the farms and fields, forests and streams beneath them.

"It *is* a beautiful world out there," she said. "I'd like to see it."

"And *I* want to test out my magic," Sumatra declared. "You know, to see what I can do with my ribbon-y halo!"

Kona nudged one of the flowers in her magical halo and laughed as it wiggled around, tickling her.

"Okay, guys," she said. "You have a point—"

"'Nuff said!" Sirocco cried. "Look out, world! Here we come!"

He fluttered his wings so hard, they buzzed. Then he zipped off.

Kona turned to Brisa and Sumatra.

"Well, *he's* sure in a hur—"

*Zzzzzippp!*

Before she could finish saying "hurry," Sumatra had darted off, too!

And Brisa? Where *was* Brisa? Kona looked around wildly. Then she glanced up to see her resting on a cloud.

"Ooh, I just *love* being magic, don't you?" Brisa called.

Before Kona could answer, Brisa disappeared into the cloud.

And just like that, Kona was all alone.

But then, one of the flowers in her halo caught her eye. Kona couldn't be sure, but it looked like the flower was *winking* at her.

"Brisa, Sumatra, and Sirocco are right. Being magic *is* fun!" Kona said to herself. She let her wings hum and darted forward. "C'mon, flowers. Let's see what we can do!"

## CHAPTER 4
# Bunches of Butterflies

$S$irocco was so excited, he couldn't fly straight.

Not that he considered flying straight to be very important. It was *much* more fun to do flips, loop-de-loops, and spirals as he flew.

He felt like he could fly all day.

Well, he could if he wasn't so *hungry*.

"I need fuel!" Sirocco announced to himself. "Something sweet. And crunchy. And juicy. Hey!"

Sirocco had just spotted a leafy tree in the center of the meadow. It was covered with big, red, shiny—

"Apples!" Sirocco shouted.

He dove down to the tree. Its fruit was almost as big as he was! Sirocco took a big bite out of one of the apples.

"Yum-o!" Sirocco chomped until he'd nibbled the apple down to its core.

"Aaah, I'm finally full," he said.

He was *so* full, in fact, that he felt kind of heavy. And sort of sleepy. And before he knew it—

Sirocco had toppled out of the apple tree— right into a bush covered with flowers!

"*Whoa!*" Sirocco cried. The impact popped several tiny butterflies right out of his halo. They flapped and fluttered indignantly for a moment. Then they recovered and flew over to the bush's purple flowers. Immediately, they began dipping into the flowers and drinking nectar.

"Hey, butterflies!" Sirocco complained. "You left a hole in my halo. Come back!"

*Fizz! Fizz! Fizz!*

Sirocco jumped. No sooner had he ordered his butterflies to return to him than new ones appeared in his halo.

"Wow!" Sirocco said. "Look at that! Not only can I pop butterflies out of my halo, I can fizz up new ones!"

Sirocco kicked some more butterflies out of his halo. *Pop, pop, pop.* And more fizzed in. *Fizz, fizz, fizz!*

"This is incredible," Sirocco cried. "I wonder how many butterflies I can make. A dozen? Fifty? A *hundred*? Why not?"

With that, Sirocco popped out a swarm of magic butterflies. It was only then that he noticed—he and his butterflies weren't alone.

There were *other* butterflies drinking nectar out of the bush's flowers. They weren't magic—they were orange and black and *real*.

"Hi, there!" Sirocco called to the closest real butterfly. It glared at Sirocco.

"Sorry to drop in so suddenly," Sirocco said with a silly grin. "What kind of bush is this?"

"This is a butterfly bush," the butterfly said brusquely.

"No *wonder* my little guys like it so much," Sirocco said.

His magic butterflies drank the nectar so hungrily, in fact, that they crowded the real butterflies out! Before long, almost all of the real butterflies got fed up and flew out of the bush altogether.

Only the butterfly who'd first spoken to Sirocco remained.

"Sorry!" Sirocco said to the butterfly. "I guess that was kind of rude."

"It was more than rude!" the butterfly said. "Don't you know what you've done? If butterflies don't drink nectar, they don't pollinate flowers. And do you know what happens when flowers don't get pollinated?"

"What?" Sirocco asked, not sure he wanted to know.

"Next year's flowers don't grow, that's what!" the butterfly answered.

"Oh, no!" Sirocco said. "What do I do?"

"*You're* the one who made this mess," the butterfly replied. "*You* figure out what to do!" Then he flew away.

Feeling guilty, Sirocco gazed at his butterflies flitting around the bush.

"Okay, guys," he commanded. "It's time to come back into my halo."

But instead of obeying, the magical creatures flew out of the bush and began searching for *more* sweet nectar.

"Oh, no!" Sirocco said again. "What do I do now?"

## CHAPTER 5
# Up, Up, and Away

Meanwhile, Brisa found herself with her head in the clouds! One moment, she was talking to Kona, the next, she was wrapped in cotton candy.

"Ooh, lovely!" Brisa cried. The cloud felt wonderful—airy and watery, all at once.

*I think Kona should stop worrying about why we have magic,* Brisa thought, *and try riding on a cloud. I'll go tell her.*

But when Brisa emerged from the cloud, Kona had disappeared!

"I wonder where she went," Brisa said.

She gazed across the meadow, but the group's leader was nowhere to be seen.

Brisa *did* see something else, though.

Something *amazing*.

It was a huge band of colors, arcing out of a distant cloud—a rainbow!

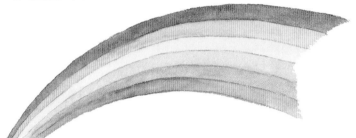

"It's the prettiest thing I've ever seen!" Brisa cried. "Besides myself, of course."

Thinking of the rainbow and her pretty self, Brisa remembered the question Kona had asked the horses: "Why are we here?"

"I think we're here to add beauty to the world!" Brisa decided. She combed a hoof through her mane. "Now, as I see it, the only thing more beautiful than a magic horse or a rainbow is a magic horse *and* a rainbow! So, I'm going to go see it up close!"

Brisa began flying with all her might.

The thing was, no matter how far and fast she flew, she didn't seem to get any closer to the rainbow!

Brisa desperately wanted to reach it.

But she was also getting tired.

"Maybe," she murmured to herself, "I could stop and rest for a minute."

At just that moment, another fluffy cloud bobbed by. It looked as soft and inviting as the first one. Brisa didn't think twice—she hopped onto the new cloud and sank into it with a grateful sigh.

And before she knew it, she'd fallen fast asleep.

. . .

Brisa didn't know how much time had gone by when she awoke with a dainty snort. All she knew was that she felt great—rested and ready to seize the rainbow!

"I just have to figure out where the rainbow is!" she said. "I can't see a thing with all this cloud in my eyes."

About to take flight, Brisa fluttered her wings gently. But she stayed right where she was!

"Okay, cloud," Brisa said sweetly. "This has been lovely, but I have to go find my rainbow now."

This time, she kicked her legs and flapped her wings at full speed ahead. But—

"*Oof!*"

Brisa was stuck!

"What's going on?" Brisa cried. Not that it did any good. The cloud had her completely fogged in. She couldn't see anything!

But she could still feel. So she poked around the cloud with her hooves. They tapped up against the jewels of her magic halo. But her jewels didn't feel quite right. Usually, they bounced around her. Now, they were absolutely still.

"Caught . . . in the cloud!" Brisa realized suddenly. "I'm trapped here! And I don't know what to do!"

"Hello? *Hellllp!*" she neighed out, all of a sudden afraid. "Can anybody hear me?"

## CHAPTER 6
# All Tied Up

As Sumatra flew across the dandelion meadow, she whinnied in excitement.

On her right was a farm with a red barn.

On her left was a duck and fish pond.

And ahead of her was a lush forest.

For a moment, Sumatra felt overwhelmed.

"I want to see everything *right now*!" she exclaimed. If she'd been standing on the ground, she would have stomped her hoof. "How do I decide what to do first?"

Just then, a tiny butterfly fluttered by.

"Hey," Sumatra said to herself, "that

looks like one of Sirocco's magic butterflies."

The little insect flew toward the forest.

"Maybe it's a sign," Sumatra said, her mood brightening. "I mean, if a magic butterfly wants to explore the forest, it *must* be an exciting place."

So, Sumatra zipped as fast as she could toward the woods, as well.

When she ducked into the forest, she gasped. It was beautiful! But as she flew deeper into the woods, it grew dark. The cool air felt heavy. And it was very quiet, but for a few bird squawks.

"Maybe," Sumatra whispered to herself, "it wasn't such a good idea to dash off without my friends."

No sooner had she uttered these words than she heard a cry from the direction of the dandelion meadow.

"Hello? *Helllllp!* Can anybody hear me?"

Sumatra reared back, neighing in fright.

Her first impulse was to fly away fast. But something stopped her. It was the thought of Kona asking, "What's our purpose?"

*I bet helping those in need is what a magic horse is supposed to do,* Sumatra realized all of a sudden.

So, even though she was scared, she called out, "Help is on the way!"

Then she began to race toward the voice. As she flew, it was all Sumatra could do to keep her little horse knees from knocking. That was, until she was distracted by a pretty glimmer of green!

Then she saw a blue shimmer and a purple gleam.

"Ooh!" she cried. "What are all those beautiful colors?"

She slowed down to look around.

"Those are my magical ribbons!" she realized with a laugh. "Flying fast sure makes them flutter!"

*"Oooh! Heeeelp!"*

The shriek was louder now. Sumatra jumped.

"Whoops, I can't forget *why* I was flying so fast," Sumatra reminded herself. "Somebody needs help!"

As she picked up speed again, Sumatra's halo of ribbons made her feel a bit braver.

*My ribbons must look pretty amazing,* Sumatra thought. She held her head high as she flew on. She imagined herself joining up again with her friends, her ribbons streaming out dramatically behind her.

"What have you been doing?" they'd ask.

"Oh, not much," she'd reply. "Just saving someone from *great peril*!"

"*Wow!*" Brisa, Kona, and Sirocco would say. "You're a hero!"

Sumatra was just starting to imagine what a medal might look like dangling from one of her pretty ribbons when, suddenly, something stopped her in mid-air!

"*Eeek!*" Sumatra shrieked as she screeched to a halt. Her legs scrabbled at the air, but something was yanking her back. "What's happened?"

She looked down at her chest, which only a moment ago had been puffed out with pride. It was now crisscrossed with . . . her own magical ribbons! They were tying her to a tree!

"Oh, no!" Sumatra cried. "I guess I was so caught up in my pretty ribbons that I didn't watch where I was going. Now my ribbons have caught up me! How am I going to be a hero now?!"

## CHAPTER 7

# Flower Power

As her friends dashed out to explore nature, Kona decided she wanted to see the farm at the edge of the dandelion meadow, about a mile from the horse paddock.

Kona loved the white curtains in every window of the yellow farmhouse, the clean red barn, and the rows of garden vegetables.

She sighed with happiness as she flew toward the farmhouse windows to take a peek inside. When she did, she gasped. A sunny-looking woman with floury hands was piping icing out of a pastry bag, putting the finishing touches on a beautiful layer cake.

Thrilled to be invisible, Kona flew inside the house for a closer look. The woman was decorating the white-frosted cake with orange icing.

*That must be a carrot cake!* Kona realized.

Kona loved carrots. She longed to taste the dessert.

*But I have no right to,* she scolded herself. *I'm not an invited guest. And I don't want to*

*risk messing up such a pretty cake.*

On the other hand, Kona remembered, she was invisible to people. And very small, at that. One bite of cake from her would be tiny. Undetectable, even.

Kona was *so* hungry. What's more, the lady had just finished frosting the cake—and had walked out of the room.

This was Kona's chance. She fluttered down to the counter and tentatively swiped one hoof through the green frosting at the *very* bottom of the cake.

"Oh, yum! *That* was delicious."

Kona wished there was a way she could thank the lady for the taste.

"But I can't very well go neigh in her ear," Kona told herself. "I'd scare her to death!"

So, reluctantly, Kona got ready to leave. As she fluttered into the air, she took one last, longing look at the cake. And gasped!

Because the spot where she'd filched the frosting had suddenly . . . sprouted flowers!

The flowers were purple, blue, and pink, *just* like the ones in her magical halo.

"Oh!" Kona squeaked. "Did I do that?"

Kona hurried back to the carrot cake. The flowers in the frosting bobbed and winked at her, as if they were saying, *"You're right. This cake is delicious!"*

"This must be my magical power," Kona realized. "I can make flowers grow on things that I touch!"

Tentatively, Kona pulled at one of the little flowers. It didn't budge.

"Uh-oh," Kona whispered.

She yanked harder at her flowers. Finally, she pulled a few of them off the cake.

"Yes!" But a moment later, Kona realized that frosting had come away *with* the flowers.

"No!" she wailed. She used her hoof to try

to smooth the surrounding frosting over the small hole, but *that* only made *more* magical flowers pop on to the cake.

"No, no, no!" Kona cried. "My magic is out of control!"

The sound of footsteps made Kona jump.

"And now the cake lady's coming back!"

Kona cried again. "She's going to see what a mess I made of her cake."

Kona desperately wanted to repair her mistake. But she didn't know how. In fact, she was pretty sure that if she tried to do anything more, she'd only make the cake worse.

So—feeling very unhappy with herself—she flew out the window.

"I think I'd better come back after I've learned how to use my powers," Kona told herself.

With that, she hung her head low and flew away from the pretty farm.

## CHAPTER 8

# Mastering Magic

Sirocco was flying above the dandelion meadow, sweaty and out of breath. He'd spent the last hour trying hard to catch his mischievous runaway butterflies. But they'd *refused* to be caught. And the *real* orange and black butterflies? They were nowhere to be seen.

"What do magic horses do?" Sirocco said, remembering Kona's question. "Well, I'm pretty sure we're *not* supposed to hog all the flower nectar and crowd perfectly nice butterflies out of their favorite meadow."

Sirocco was also certain that Kona would be disappointed in him when she found out what he'd done.

He heaved a big sigh. As he did, one of his butterflies flew up and landed right on his nose! Sirocco gasped. Then he tried to swipe the butterfly back into his halo. Of course, it dodged his hoof and took off for the forest.

"Hey!" Sirocco called after the butterfly. "You've got some nerve! Get back here!"

The butterfly turned and winked at him with its wings. Then, it darted off again.

"That does it!" Sirocco said to himself. "If I don't catch *any* other butterflies today, I'm going to nab *that* one!"

He took off after the butterfly.

It zipped toward the sky. Sirocco followed.

It dove to the ground. Sirocco did the same.

Finally, the butterfly flew through a low-hanging cloud. Sirocco chased after it.

"*Ow!*" Sirocco's head had butted right into something warm and silky, and not at *all* cloud-like. Sirocco heard a tinkling sound, and then, a voice!

"Oooh! That hurt!"

The cloud was so thick and white that Sirocco couldn't see whom he'd hit. But that didn't matter—he recognized the voice!

"Brisa?!" he exclaimed.

"Sirocco?" said Brisa's voice. "You've come to save me! My hero!"

"Um, actually, I came to find my escaped butterfly," Sirocco said. "Have you seen it?"

"I haven't seen *anything* for a while now," Brisa complained. "I've been trapped in this cloud. My magic jewels have got me pinned! Hey, did you say one of your butterflies *escaped*?"

"Yeah!" Sirocco said. He sat down in the comfy cloud. "Only, it wasn't just one. It was more like a hundred."

"A *hundred*?!"

"Yup," Sirocco said. "I popped them out of my halo. It was fun . . . at the time."

He perked up.

"Hey, maybe that's what you should do," he suggested to Brisa. "Kick your jewels out of your halo. Then you won't be pinned anymore."

"Oh, no!" Brisa said. "I love my jewels, even if they're a bit unmanageable. They're so pretty."

"No worries!" Sirocco said. "More will fizz up in their place. I'll show you."

Before Brisa could say anything else, Sirocco jumped up and started bucking and kicking. He enjoyed the sound his hooves made as they kicked the jewels out of Brisa's halo: *Clink! Pop! Clink!*

Within a minute, Sirocco had popped Brisa right out of the cloud! She burst into the air with a joyful whinny. Her magic halo was clear and empty, but only for a moment. Then . . .

*Fizz, fizz, fizz, fizz!*

A bunch of new jewels appeared around her.

"*Whee!*" Brisa cried. "I'm free *and* still pretty!"

She was admiring her fresh new jewels when something flew up to admire *her*. It was Sirocco's butterfly! As it fluttered around her sparkly halo, Sirocco spotted it.

"Hey!" he bellowed. "C'MERE, YOU!"

He leaped at the butterfly. But once again, the magic insect dodged him.

"Aw, man!" Sirocco said.

"Sirocco," Brisa suggested gently, "maybe you need to change your approach."

"What do you mean?" Sirocco asked.

"Maybe instead of chasing your butterflies and yelling at them," Brisa said, "you should just try talking to them. You know—nicely?"

Sirocco glowered at Brisa.

"Well, if you think you could do better," he offered, "be my guest!"

"Oh, don't be mad," Brisa said sweetly.

Together, the two tiny horses flew into the forest. As soon as they ducked beneath the treetops, Brisa gasped! There were magic butterflies everywhere—and most of them were dipping into the forest's wildflowers.

"Sirocco!" Brisa said. "How many butter-flies did you set free?"

"Hey, it was fun!" Sirocco defended him-self. "I didn't tease you for napping in a cloud, did I?"

Brisa giggled.

"Okay, you have a point."
Then she turned toward the butterflies and called out, "Oh, excuse me? Little butterflies? Sirocco would love it if you'd come back inside his halo. You don't mind, do you?"

The butterflies ignored her. Completely.

Brisa was puzzled. "Maybe I should get closer to them."

She flew over to a cluster of butterflies circling a tree trunk.

"Come here, little butterflies," she crooned. "I'll take you back to Sirocco."

The butterflies flew toward her. Brisa held her breath—until the butterflies flew right past her!

"Oh! That was rude," Brisa scolded. She flew after the butterflies.

They darted away from her again. So Brisa flew after them faster.

Finally, Brisa screeched to a halt in the air and shouted, "Hey! GET BACK HERE!!!!"

Sirocco burst out laughing.

"Haaa-haa-haa! Gee, Brisa. Maybe if you tried talking to the butterflies instead of chasing them and yelling at them . . ."

Brisa's pink-tinged face went even pinker. But before she could retort, a loud voice echoed through the woods.

*"Hellllp!"*

Brisa and Sirocco looked at each other in alarm.

"That's Sumatra!" Brisa cried. "I'm sure!"

"Let's go!" Sirocco said.

Together, the magic horses zinged through the forest, following Sumatra's cries. When they reached her, Sumatra was tied to a tree trunk, her silvery face streaked with tears.

"Oh!" Brisa cried. "Don't worry, Sumatra! We're here to save you."

Sirocco immediately began working at the knots in Sumatra's ribbons with his teeth.

"Thanks, but as soon as you help me," Sumatra breathed, "head to the dandelion meadow. Somebody there needs help, too!"

Brisa and Sirocco looked at each other. Brisa blushed again.

"Well, that's very sweet of you to want to

help," Brisa said, "but that voice in the dandelion meadow was kind of . . . me. You see, my magic jewels got me caught in a cloud."

"Just like my magic ribbons tangled me up," Sumatra said.

Sirocco untied the last ribbon, setting Sumatra free.

"What would you damsels in distress do

without me?" Sirocco teased.

"Okay, I'm going to choose to ignore that," Sumatra said, as she stretched out her wings, "only because I saw about fifty of your magic butterflies fly by before you arrived."

She and Brisa giggled while Sirocco hung his head.

"What am I going to do?" he moaned.

"Maybe we should go find Kona," Sumatra suggested. Idly, she shook away something tickling her ear. "I bet she'll know what to do."

"Yeah," Sirocco complained. "She'll give me a big long lecture, that's what she'll do."

"Oh, Sirocco," Sumatra said, shaking the tickle off her other ear now. "Kona's not *that* bossy."

"Hey!" she said. "Why am I so ticklish?"

Brisa and Sirocco glanced at Sumatra, then gasped in disbelief.

"My butterflies!" Sirocco whispered.

Dozens of butterflies were lined up on Sumatra's fluttery ribbons.

"Hey!" Brisa whispered suddenly. Butterflies were poking at her gems, too, as if they thought they were delicious flowers. Within minutes, at least a hundred butterflies had flocked to Sumatra's and Brisa's pretty halos.

Sirocco gulped. Now was his chance to get his butterflies back. But to do so, he'd have to act very un-Sirocco-like.

He nickered softly and whispered, "Here, guys. C'mon home."

And just like that, the butterflies flew from the ribbons and jewels into Sirocco's halo.

*Fizz, fizz, fizz, fizz!*

In an instant, Sirocco's halo was packed.

"Better to have my butterflies crowding me," he told Brisa and Sumatra with a big grin, "than crowding the real butterflies off the flowers."

"And more good news," Sumatra said,

also grinning. "I think you've saved yourself from a lecture from Kona!"

"Let's go find her!" Brisa declared. "I think we've explored enough for one day."

"Yeah!" Sirocco agreed.

The three horses zipped out of the forest and winged their way toward the farm where they'd last seen Kona.

As she flew, Sumatra was careful not to go too fast, and her ribbons stayed untangled.

Brisa flew (pretty much) in a straight line. And her jewels didn't snag on anything.

Sirocco kicked and bucked a little more carefully than usual—and none of his butter-flies popped out of his halo.

Now, if only he'd also remembered to watch where he was going. . . .

Thump!

"*Ow!*" Sirocco cried. He'd crashed right into another flying creature!

A creature covered in purple, pink, and blue flowers.

The creature shook its head hard.

*Pop, pop, pop, pop!*

Flowers went flying, revealing . . .

"Kona!" Sirocco, Sumatra, and Brisa gasped together.

Kona looked at her three friends with wide, startled eyes. Then she peered down to see where her flowers were landing.

"Oh, no!" she cried. Some of the flowers landed on the front windshield of a truck in the farmhouse's driveway. They attached themselves to the window with a sucking sound. Other flowers twined themselves around a few tree trunks.

"First, I mess up a beautiful carrot cake inside the farmhouse, now this!" Kona cried. "I just can't control these magical flowers!"

Her friends exchanged a quick glance, then ducked their heads to keep themselves from laughing.

Unfortunately, they failed miserably.

"I don't think it's very funny," Kona said, looking hurt. "I've got too much magic!"

"That's what's so funny," Brisa explained. "Our magic got all of us into jams today. We

 68

were sure you were going to lecture us!"

Kona looked shocked. And then she began shaking with laughter, too!

"And here I thought being magic was going to be so awesome," Sirocco said.

Kona gazed down at all her misplaced flowers. Then she said, "Hold on, I want to try something."

She flew down to a nearby wooden fence and galloped along its top rail. When she reached the end, there wasn't one misplaced flower on the rail. Her flowers had stayed where they were supposed to—in her halo.

"How'd you do that?" Sirocco breathed.

"The same way I knew my name," Kona said. "I just concentrated on what I wanted to do. When I control my flowers in my mind, it seems I control them for real, too!"

"Wow!" Sumatra said. "I'm going to try that, too."

"Me, too!" Brisa and Sirocco said at the same time.

Kona rose up and called her fellow horses together. "Group nose nuzzle, everyone," she said.

Then Kona whinnied and said, "Our magic *is* awesome. I have a feeling it's going to take us on a lot more adventures!"

## *The End—of the Day*

The sun was setting and the tiny, winged horses were tired. Sure that they were still invisible to people, they flew to the cozy porch of the yellow farmhouse, with the big red barn, to take a rest. They landed on the porch swing and made themselves comfy.

"It's been the busiest day ever," Sumatra said with a yawn.

"What do you mean?" Sirocco said. "It's been our only day ever!"

"I wonder what will happen tomorrow," Brisa said dreamily.

Kona gazed out at the darkening horizon.

"And I wonder . . ." But Kona stopped

herself before she could finish her thought. "Oh, never mind. I don't want to be serious when you're all so happy."

"No," Sumatra said. "All of us should say what we think. Go ahead, Kona."

"Well," Kona began, "we figured out how to control our magic today. But we still didn't learn what we're supposed to do with it."

"You're right," Sirocco said. "But can't we deal with that question tomorrow?"

But before Kona could say anything else, the porch's screen door opened. The winged horses fell silent as a young girl stepped out of the house and headed for the porch swing!

"*Eeek!*" Brisa squeaked.

The horses darted away from the swing seconds before the girl sat down. They flew up to hover beneath the porch ceiling.

"Hey!" Sirocco said. "That's the little girl that we saw in the meadow this morning!"

"You're right," Kona said. "She must live here! And the lady who made the carrot cake must be her mother."

"Look at her," Sumatra said softly. "She still looks sad and lonely."

"Poor thing," Brisa sighed.

Suddenly, Kona gasped. "Wait a minute," she said. "I know the answer!"

"The answer to what?" Sirocco asked.

"To why we're here!" Kona said. "Maybe it's to make people like her feel better."

She pointed at the girl.

"But how?" Brisa wondered.

"With our magic, of course," Kona said.

The four horses looked at each other. Without saying another word, they knew just what to do.

·   ·   ·

A few minutes later, a woman's voice rang out from inside the house.

"Leanna! It's almost time for bed."

The girl, now kneeling on the porch swing, looked sadly at the sky. And the horses, hovering nearby, looked at each other.

"The little girl is named Leanna," Brisa said. "Oh, what a pretty name."

"Leanna!" Leanna's mother called again. "If you come inside lickety-split, you can have carrot cake before you go to bed. I made it today. Somehow some tiny little flowers got stuck in it—"

Kona cringed!

"—but it still tastes yummy," Leanna's mother added.

"*Whew!*" Kona whispered in relief.

"Well . . . okay," Leanna called back.

She stood up and started for the porch door. Right before she opened it, she saw a reflection of herself in one of the windows.

"What's this?" she gasped as her hands

flew up to her neck.

The horses tried not to make a sound.

"It's the prettiest necklace ever!" Leanna cried. She stood on her tiptoes to get a better look at herself in the window's reflection. Then she fingered her new necklace: three charms strung on a shimmery silver ribbon. One of the charms was a pink jewel. Another was a shiny butterfly. And the last was a sweet purple flower.

"I bet I know who gave me this necklace," Leanna whispered happily. "Those little winged horses! The ones I blew out of the dandelion!"

"She blew us out of a dandelion?!" Sirocco whispered to Kona, Sumatra, and Brisa. "So *that's* where we came from!"

"Ooh, how nice!" Brisa said. "Dandelions are so soft and pretty."

"Shhh," Kona cautioned, though she was smiling as much as the rest of them. "Leanna's still talking."

"I bet the flying horses are still nearby," Leanna said. "My little Wind Dancers."

"Wind Dancers?" Sumatra said. "Oh, I like that name!"

"It's perfect!" Kona breathed.

"Because we dance on the wind!" Brisa cried, spinning through the air.

"Leanna!"

"Coming!" Leanna called as she ran inside. "Mom! You'll never guess what I just got . . ."

As Leanna's voice trailed off, the horses

smiled at each other.

"We used our magic to make a lonely girl happy," Kona said proudly.

"I wish we could do that again," Brisa replied with a happy sigh.

"I bet we'll get our chance," Kona added, with one last glance through the porch door.

Here's a sneak preview of *Wind Dancers* Book 2:

# Horse Happy

## CHAPTER 1
## Home, Apple-Sweet Home

The Wind Dancers couldn't believe it—their first magical day on earth was coming to a close. And they had been *busy*.

They'd explored the meadows, forests, and farms of their new world. . . .

. . . Now the horses were flying into the darkening sky, enjoying their first sunset, and feeling their wings get heavy.

"I can't *wait* to get to bed," Brisa said, her pretty brown eyes looking sleepy.

"Me, too," Sumatra added. She stretched her front hooves and yawned a big yawn.

"Some shut-eye sounds awesome," Sirocco agreed. "There's just one problem: We *have* no beds!"

This stopped Brisa in mid-flight.

"Oh, *no*! I never thought about that!" she cried. "We don't have a home!"

Kona, of course, was quick to comfort everyone.

"There are plenty of cozy places we can stay," she assured her friends. "We can go back to Leanna's farmhouse and sleep on the porch. Or we can nest in the barn. Or we can make beds out of soft leaves in the garden. We'll be fine for tonight."